I Like My Town

Characters

 Red Group

 Blue Group

 Purple Group

 All

Setting A town

by Francisco Blane

My Picture Words

 house

 playground

 school

 street

My Sight Words

has

here

I

is

like

my

My  is here.

house

 My has  .

house   bricks

 I like my .

house

My  is here.

street

 My  has .

street   trees

 I like my .

street

My  is here.

playground

 My  has .

playground   swings

 I like my .

playground

My  is here.

school

 My  has  .

school · books

 I like my  .

school

I like my  !

town

The End